W9-BYD-383

T. Ripley

Rabble Rousers

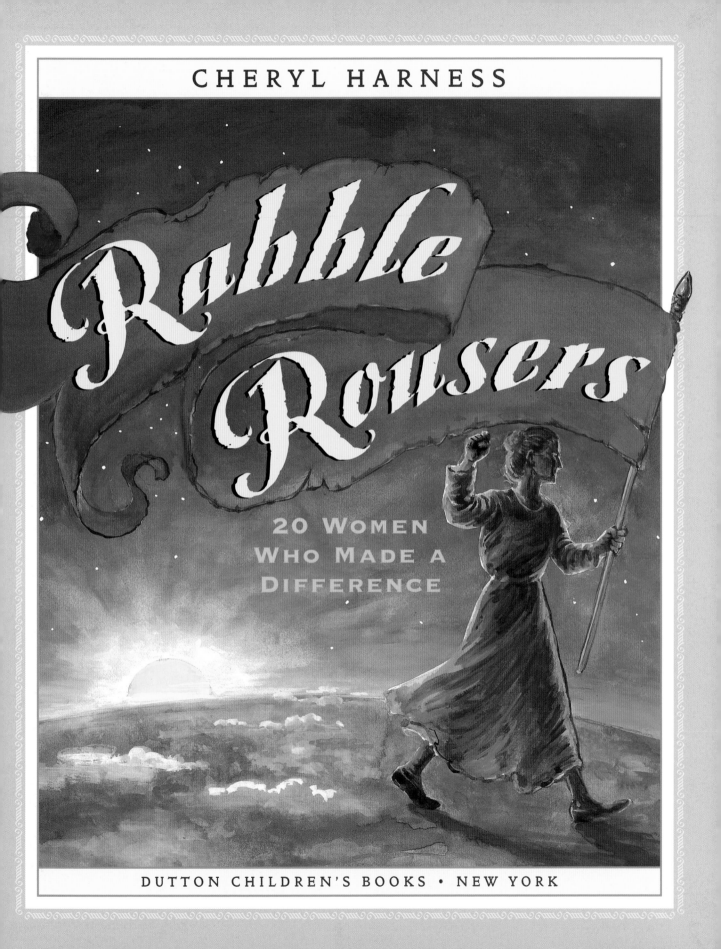

CHERYL HARNESS

Rabble Rousers

20 Women Who Made a Difference

DUTTON CHILDREN'S BOOKS · NEW YORK

To my friends and long-gone mother-line:
Elaine, Eula, Emma, and . . .

Copyright © 2003 by Cheryl Harness
All rights reserved.

CIP Data is available.

Published in the United States 2003 by Dutton Children's Books,
a division of Penguin Young Readers Group
345 Hudson Street, New York, New York 10014
www.penguin.com

Designed by Alyssa Morris and Ellen M. Lucaire
Art direction by Sara Reynolds

Printed in China
First Edition
2 3 4 5 6 7 8 9 10
ISBN 0-525-47035-2

CONTENTS

The future depends entirely on what each of us does every day.
—GLORIA STEINEM

Once a person steps into the circle of those who take responsibility for the happy operation of the community . . . the magic of community begins.
—DORIS HADDOCK

This book is about twenty big-hearted women who dared to try to change the world. Misery and unfairness inspired them. Anger spurred them. They wanted to rouse the people—wake them up to what they might not see. They wanted to remake, reeducate, redeem, and reform. Each of these women spoke out loud her personal vision of a land in which the powerless would have an equal chance at the "unalienable Rights" spelled out in the great manifesto of the republic of the United States of America: "Life, Liberty, and the Pursuit of Happiness."

Their Happiness-chasing methods landed them in trouble. Folks said they were unladylike, dangerous, crazy, and radical—and they meant that last word to sting. "Too extreme" is what they meant. But look it up and you'll find that *radical* comes from a word that means "root," as in the root of the issue. The foundation, the source, the fundamental basics. You could use it in a sentence like this, for example: Our republic is based upon the radical principles of freedom, justice, and the idea that power lives in "We the people."

To that, each of these women would say, "Amen."

Ann Lee

FEBRUARY 29, 1736
Manchester, England

SEPTEMBER 8, 1784
Watervliet, New York

*"I put my hands to work
and my heart to God."*

You can still see the fortunate folk of 18th-century England in oil paintings: ladies with their rosy children and silk-stockinged husbands. They look as if they lived far from the grimy, smelly city where pale children worked long days in the textile mills, making the mill owners rich enough to live in big houses and have their portraits painted.

One of those mill workers was eight-year-old Ann Lee. Her twelve-hour workdays set her to dreaming of a better world. Years later, after she married and had four babies who died one by one, Ann dove deep into her faith. Blue-eyed Ann Lee became a seeker after truth and purity in a miserable world. What she found would turn her world upside down.

Ann found comfort in the "Shaking Quakers," a group of peace-loving men and women who were literally moved by their worship—they danced, shouted, and sang. In their eyes God was both male and female, and anyone—even a woman—could

preach. In 1770 Ann told poverty-stricken, passionate followers about a "glorious klang of being," her vision of a heaven on earth where people would live and work together, sharing equally. They would live in "virgin purity," doing nothing that might make babies or distract from their love of God.

Ann's ideas were too extreme for some people, who chased her, beat her, even jailed her. Finally, she and eight "Shakers" left England and sailed to where they might worship in peace: America. They founded their first colony, Niskeyuna, near Albany, New York, in 1776. It was a hard, war-shadowed beginning for the little band of believers. The fact that they were pacifists made some people afraid that the Shakers might be British spies! Still, people were steadily drawn to the little woman who wore herself out walking all over New England, inspiring and infuriating listeners.

Mother Ann planted the seed of a harmonious society that grew—despite the fact that Shakers did not have babies—to more than 6,000 "brothers and sisters" in nineteen villages from Maine to Kentucky in the years before the Civil War. The numbers have since dwindled to a tiny few who keep "Mother's Wisdom": that simplicity is God's gift, and God is work done well. A simple chair made with care might be seen as a prayer. Shakers invented many tools to speed their work: the flat broom, clothespin, washing machine, circular saw, potato peeler, and more—all testaments of a lively faith inspired by a bold, illiterate woman. Ann Lee tried to create heaven on earth, then passed from the earth when she was 48 years old, in the fall of 1784. No portrait of her was ever painted.

Frances Wright

SEPTEMBER 6, 1795
Dundee, Scotland

DECEMBER 13, 1852
Cincinnati, Ohio

"I have wedded the cause of human improvement, staked on it my fortune, my reputation, my life."

In the early nineteenth century, when Americans got together to celebrate the glorious Fourth of July, they did so with pride, and lots of food, drink, and racket. Then a highly esteemed gent in a tall collar would make an Independence Day oration. On July 4, 1828, the citizens of New Harmony listened to a native of Scotland give a corker of a speech about America. But the native was no gentleman. Frances Wright told them that "liberty means, not the mere voting at elections, but the free and fearless exercise of the mental exercise of the mental faculties. . . ."

Free people thinking freely and people living their best lives: those ideas were twins as far as Fanny Wright was concerned, ever since she was a girl. Shortly before she turned twenty-three, Fanny had set out for the country that symbolized all her romantic ideals about liberty and tolerance. Except for the shockingly rude reality of slavery, Fanny loved the United States so much that in 1821, she wrote a glowing book, *Views of Society and Manners in America,* about her experiences there.

The Marquis de Lafayette, the French hero of the Revolutionary War, admired her book so much that he took Fanny to meet his old friends Thomas Jefferson and James Madison. They saw her as a champion of their revolutionary ideals. The old men predicted future trouble and violence because of slavery. Fanny was determined to find a peaceful way of ending this "foul blot" on her beloved America.

In 1825, in Tennessee, she started a community called Nashoba where slaves could learn the skills they would need as they earned their freedom. Sickness and inexperience unraveled the experiment by 1827. Then Fanny Wright traveled all around America, speaking to huge crowds who came to see the shocking novelty of a female speaking in public. They heard the white-gowned Scotswoman's even more shocking views against slavery and mind-shackling churches. She spoke out about how women were legally chained—in cruel marriages, with no vote, no chance for equal education, and no choice about having babies. Folks rioted. They set off smoke bombs to clear out her lecture halls.

Restless Fanny edited newspapers, married, traveled between France and America, and kept talking about free education and the rights of working people. As she and her adopted country got older, fewer and fewer came to hear her speak. But her belief in the republic founded on the Fourth of July was a torch that never burned out. To her, the republic of the United States was a nation of patriots "capable of enlarging all minds and bettering all hearts." To her, America was the best hope of the world.

Emma Hart Willard

FEBRUARY 23, 1787
Berlin, Connecticut

APRIL 15, 1870
Troy, New York

> *"Genuine learning has ever been said to give polish to man; why then should it not bestow added charm on women?"*

*E*mma Hart's father had advanced views. He wanted his seventeen children, including his girls, to have book learning. Emma must have inherited her father's belief in the importance of education. By the time she was seventeen, Emma was teaching school in her hometown. Later she taught at a "female academy" in Vermont and eventually married Dr. John Willard of Middlebury. There was a college in the town, and Emma got the chance to study the geometry, algebra, science, history, geography, Latin, and Greek textbooks that were available to the male students but not to her young ladies.

In Emma's day, most people figured that girls didn't need to know too much more than how to read, clean house, look after the children, and get supper on the table. This was the "woman's sphere," which existed in a notch above children and below men. If a young lady came from a family with money, then she might learn to embroider, speak French, make some music, and manage the servants. There were plenty of earnest fussbudgets who thought that learning "hard" subjects might hurt girls' brains—and that it was against God's will. Radical Emma Willard was determined to change the world, one ringleted head at a time, in a school of her own. It was 1814.

As the seventy students at her Middlebury Female Seminary wrapped their hungry minds around their courses, Emma Hart Willard mapped out a Plan for Improving Female Education. It would "bring its subjects to the perfection of their moral, intellectual and physical nature . . ." In 1818, she sent her plan to the New York legislature and to Governor DeWitt Clinton. He had advanced views about "internal improvements," such as the mighty Erie Canal men were digging clear across the state. What could be more internally improving than making citizens smarter? He gave Mrs. Willard a charter—but no money—to open a school for women in Waterford. Folks shook their heads. Educated women? It wasn't natural! "They'll be educating the cows next," a farmer was heard to say. Still, in 1821, the town of Troy, New York, voted $4,000 for a building, and the Troy Female Seminary was born, the first to offer women advanced studies.

Ninety students were the first of hundreds who would take what they learned and pass it on as schoolteachers (a profession that was, in those days, becoming fully possible and respectable for women) or as influential citizens with advanced views. Soon there would be public high schools for girls in Boston and New York City, and in Oberlin, Ohio, giving smart, bold women a chance to go to college.

Emma Hart Willard wrote poems as well as history and geography textbooks, and she traveled thousands of miles to talk to thousands of people about the infinite possibilities in the minds of girls—if only the doors were opened.

Sojourner Truth

c.1797
Ulster County, New York

NOVEMBER 26, 1883
Battle Creek, Michigan

"I could work as much and eat as much as a man—when I could get it—and bear the lash as well! And ain't I a woman?"

Betsey and James gave their new baby daughter the name of a queen, Isabella. "Belle's" last name, Baumfree, was the name of one of the masters who owned them. By the time the politicians in her home state of New York made slavery illegal, in 1827, Belle was a wife, mom, milkmaid, field hand, cook, washerwoman, and doer of just about everything that needed doing. She'd been owned and beaten by a succession of masters. The new law was no guarantee that her owner was eager to emancipate his valuable "property," so Belle had to commit self-liberation. She escaped!

Belle was six feet tall and steely strong, with a deep, powerful voice. She was strong on the inside, too, thanks to her prayer and deep meditations. She was working as a house servant in New York City when it came to her that she was to "sojourn" (journey) across the land and speak the truth. In June 1843, with twenty-five cents in her pocket and a new name, Sojourner Truth set out walking. She set out to be a preacher.

Folks threw mean words at her, but she would not be swayed. They hurt her with fists and swift kicks, but she kept on. "Children," she'd say, "I talk to God and he talks to me." She talked to all who would listen about the rights of those who'd been born low on America's ladder: girls, blacks, the poor. Old Sojourner was wise in the ways of all three.

"Children," she'd say, "where there is so much racket there must be something out of kilter. I think that 'twixt the Negroes of the South and the women at the North, all talking about rights, the white men will be in a fix pretty soon." By the time she got to "old Sojourner ain't got nothing more to say," she was met with tears and clapping hands, black and white. People bought copies of her life story, *The Narrative of Sojourner Truth*, which illiterate Sojourner had dictated in 1850, and postcards with her picture on them. They financed her mission to melt hard hearts, maybe change the nation's mind a little about how women and blacks were treated.

Sojourner Truth shared platforms with the equally eloquent Frederick Douglass. She raised funds for supplies for black Union soldiers and cared for them when they

were sick or hurt in battle. To see about better lives for freed slaves, she met with President Lincoln in the White House. Nearly seventy-year-old Sojourner the Freedom Rider desegregated the streetcars of Washington, D.C., in the fall of 1865.

She sojourned on, speaking out for women's rights and opportunities in the West for freed slaves until she settled down with her family in Battle Creek, Michigan, in 1875. There old Sojourner finally came to rest.

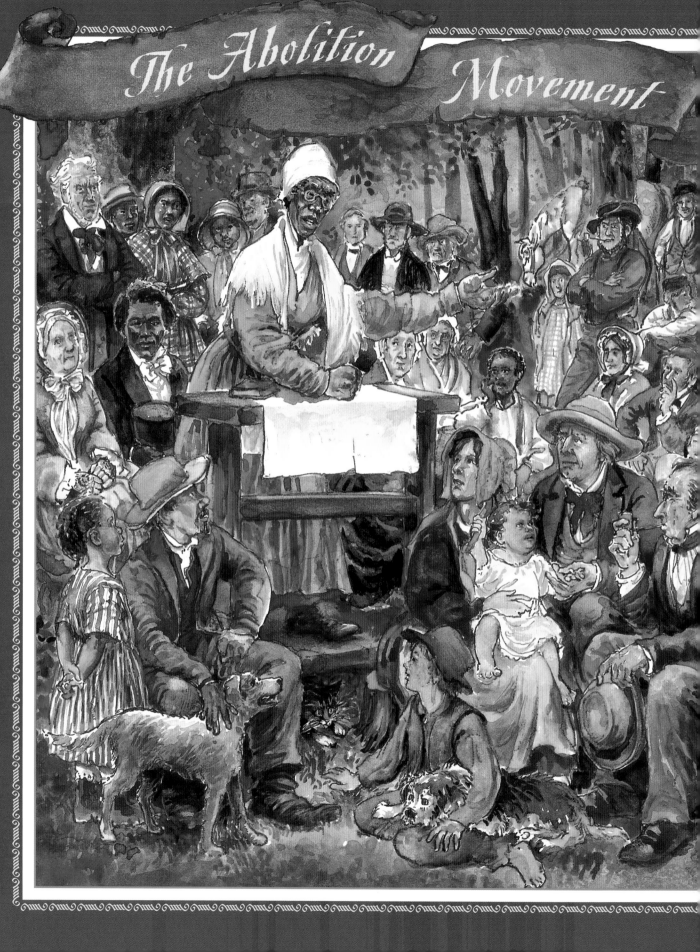

The Abolition Movement

EARLY 1600S ✤ First Africans are brought to work in the English colonies in North America.

1750 ✤ Approximately 200,000 slaves and perhaps 40,000 free blacks live in America.

MARCH 5, 1770 ✤ Black American Crispus Attucks is killed in the Boston Massacre, a street fight/protest between Colonials and British soldiers.

1775–1783 ✤ Nearly 5,000 black Americans, such as Peter Salem of Massachusetts, fight on the side of the Colonials in the Revolutionary War for Independence.

JUNE 21, 1788 ✤ U.S. Constitution is ratified. Slavery is allowed in the home of the free. Slaves are not considered to be citizens.

1817 ✤ The American Colonization Society is founded on the idea that free blacks would volunteer to go back to Africa.

1821 ✤ American colony of Liberia is founded in Africa.

1827 ✤ First black-owned and -operated newspaper, *Freedom's Journal*, is published.

1831 ✤ Preacher Nat Turner leads the best known of nearly 200 slave revolts in Southampton County, Virginia.

1839 ✤ Cinque leads a slave mutiny aboard the *Amistad*.

1847 ✤ Frederick Douglass begins his abolition newspaper, *The North Star*.

1849 ✤ Harriet Tubman escapes slavery in Maryland. She will help more than 300 slaves escape to freedom.

1850 ✤ Congress passes the Fugitive Slave Law: Runaways may be captured in the North, returned to the South.

1852 ✤ Harriet Beecher Stowe publishes *Uncle Tom's Cabin*, a best-seller about the cruelties of slavery.

1854 ✤ Kansas-Nebraska Act whips up tensions even more: People in new territories can vote whether to become slave or free.

1857 ✤ Dred Scott decision: Supreme Court says no black, slave or free, can be a U.S. citizen, and Congress shall not stop the spread of slavery.

1859 ✤ John Brown leads an abolitionist group in an attack and capture of the U.S. arsenal at Harpers Ferry.

1861–1865 ✤ The Civil War. Approximately 40,000 black troops of the 200,000 who fought for the Union died during the war.

DECEMBER 1865 ✤ The 13th Amendment to the U.S. Constitution officially ends slavery throughout the nation. Four million black Americans are freed.

Mary Ann Shadd Cary

OCTOBER 9, 1823
Wilmington, Delaware

JUNE 5, 1893
Washington, D.C.

*"It is better to wear out
than to rust out."*

While Sojourner Truth put a human face on the tragedy of slavery, Mary Ann Shadd's way was to edit a newspaper. She was the first African-American woman to do so.

Mary Ann was born to parents who opened their home many a night to desperate folks running from slavery in the South. Although Abraham and Harriett Shadd were free, their thirteen children couldn't go to school in their state of Delaware because they were black. Mary Ann was educated at a Quaker school in Pennsylvania, but as soon as she graduated, in 1839, she returned to Wilmington and began teaching African-American students. She was only sixteen, but she was plenty determined and plenty old enough to share her knowledge.

As if the world weren't unfair enough, the Fugitive Slave Law was passed in 1850. Slaves who'd managed to get to the free states up North were to be returned to their owners in the South. And bounty-hunting "slave catchers" weren't too particular about who they caught: any dark-skinned person would do. Mary Ann Shadd and thousands of African-Americans went to Canada, out of harm's way.

Mary Ann helped to start a weekly newspaper, *The Provincial Freeman*, full of information for blacks looking to build new lives in the far North. She wrote, taught, and found time to meet and marry Thomas Cary. To raise awareness and money for the paper, she returned to the States to make speeches about the "noble deeds and heroism of the colored American." Later on, Mary Ann Shadd Cary became a recruiting officer for the Union army. Black soldiers in Federal blue showed their heroism in the Civil War, which brought slavery to an end at last in 1865.

As far as Mrs. Cary and millions of others were concerned, freedom was one thing—one glorious thing. Justice was another proposition. Blacks and women had no say in the democracy, because they had no vote. Suffrage still had to be pried out of many a clenched fist.

Mary Ann Shadd Cary became a mother, then a widow. All the while she kept writing and speaking for full civil equality. By day she was a school principal in Washington, D.C. At night she went to Howard University. By the time she turned sixty, in 1883, she'd organized women whose goal was the right to vote: the Colored Women's Progressive Franchise Association. She was the second African-American woman in history (Charlotte E. Ray was the first, in 1872) to earn a law degree and the right to practice her profession. Mary Ann Shadd Cary used her life to make the world a fairer place, until she used it up in the summer of 1893.

Elizabeth Cady Stanton

NOVEMBER 12, 1815
Johnstown, New York

OCTOBER 26, 1902
New York, New York

*"The right is ours.
Have it we must. Use it we will."*

G rowing up, Lizzie fizzed with indignation over the fact that her father, Judge Cady, wished that she were a boy. After Lizzie graduated with honors from Emma Willard's Female Seminary in Troy, New York, she married Henry Stanton. At that time, this meant that she was giving him the keys to her life. If a married woman had a job, the husband got the paycheck. If she inherited a farm or money, he got those, too. Their children were legally his and only his. A woman could not be on a jury or sign a contract. Lizzie fizzed.

The young couple agreed on two things: Lizzie Stanton would not promise to obey Mr. Stanton, and they both believed that slavery was hideous. In 1840, they sailed to London for the World's Anti-Slavery Convention. Mrs. Stanton could only listen. Guess why.

Elizabeth Cady Stanton and another woman, Quaker minister Lucretia Mott, eventually organized their own meeting, in 1848. More than 300 people, including

Frederick Douglass, showed up at the very first Woman's Rights Convention in Seneca Falls, New York. They heard a tiny, thirty-two-year-old mother reading her "Declaration of Sentiments." She improved on Thomas Jefferson's words: ". . . all men and women are created equal." She demanded, in public, voting rights for women. Outrageous! Unheard of! Elizabeth Cady Stanton sparked a thought revolution that ended up winning the right to vote for all the girl-born citizens of the nation.

Nearly three years later, on May 13, 1851, the women's rights movement began in earnest with a fateful meeting on a Seneca Falls street corner. Amelia Bloomer, the journalist best known for her efforts to free women from heavy skirts, introduced two of her friends to each other. The full-trousered "Bloomer" costume all three would wear soon fell out of fashion. The partnership between Lizzie Cady Stanton and Susan B. Anthony would last fifty years.

Lizzie and Susan, the tireless traveling speaker, aimed their souls at reforming the world. "I forged the thunderbolts," said Lizzie, and Susan fired them. They worked for temperance (against drunkenness) and abolition. They got New York lawmakers to give married women equal rights to their own wages and children. They faced many setbacks and mixed blessings in their battles for suffrage—the right to vote. The 15th Amendment to the Constitution allowed black men to vote—glorious day! Women could *not*. Abolitionists such as Sojourner Truth, Lucretia Mott, and Harriet Tubman all had to accept victory mixed with the bitter business of being passed over.

Furious Lizzie and Susan started the National Woman Suffrage Association, aimed at changing U.S. law and winning equal pay for women and an eight-hour workday. Mrs. Stanton wrote a woman suffrage amendment and got it introduced in the Congress in 1878. It would be voted down every year for the rest of her life.

Elizabeth Cady Stanton didn't look like a radical, but that's what people thought she was. Just beneath her curls, a tough brain crackled with opinions on anything that kept women down or got in the way of independent thinking, including marriage and religion. Eyes dim, body thick and slow, bold mind fizzing bright, Lizzie Cady Stanton died when she was 87 years old. Her loyal friend Susan wrote, "It is an awful hush."

FEBRUARY 15, 1820
Adams, Massachusetts

MARCH 13, 1906
Rochester, New York

Susan B. Anthony

"Failure is impossible."

Many women opposed the idea of suffrage. They thought that politics was unrefined and noisy reformers were no credit to their sex. People made fun of spinster Susan B. Anthony, the stern-faced dynamo, and Elizabeth Cady Stanton, the lacy dumpling of an old lady with outlandish opinions. But when Mrs. Stanton died in 1902, the newspapers remarked upon the end of a friendship between the "noted women." Lizzie had stirred up Susan, who stirred up the world. Fifty years of pushing had won them respect, but it still hadn't won women the constitutional right to vote. Eighty-two-year-old Susan B. Anthony kept right on working.

By the time the 31-year-old Quaker schoolteacher met Mrs. Stanton, Miss Anthony had already met many of the temperance and abolition bigshots of her day, including Frederick Douglass, the orator, and William Lloyd Garrison, the Boston publisher. Susan was bristling with energy and busting to get involved.

She went everywhere, circulating petitions, holding meetings, giving speeches. She climbed aboard stagecoaches, steamboats, and railroad cars to go wherever people would gather. Susan and Elizabeth published a newspaper, *The Revolution*, between 1868 and 1870. Miss Anthony organized parades, conventions, and action groups. She worked with other groups, such as the huge Woman's Christian Temperance Union (WCTU), the National Association of Colored Women, and the American Woman Suffrage Association, formed by Lucy Stone in 1869. In 1892 "the Invincible" Susan became president of the merged National American Woman Suffrage Association (NAWSA).

Susan helped write four thick volumes of history about the fight for the vote. The presidential election of 1872 made for a lively chapter. Victoria C. Woodhull, a former stock-broker and fortune-teller who called for "free love" and the overthrow "of this bogus Republic," ran for the highest office in the land. She made plenty of headlines, and so did Susan B. Anthony when she attempted to vote (for Republican Ulysses S. Grant—definitely not Miss Woodhull!). For this, the educated, 52-year-old citizen was arrested, taken to jail, tried, found guilty, and fined $100 for participating in the democratic government of her country. "I will never pay a dollar of your unjust penalty," said the woman whose face would appear on a dollar coin in 1979, the first woman to be pictured on U.S. currency.

After she had lost her best friend, Mrs. Stanton, the frail, silvery Susan B. Anthony kept traveling and speaking. "Aunt Susan" worked with young colleagues, such as the Reverend Anna Howard Shaw and Carrie Chapman Catt. It would be left to them and a legion of "nieces" to finish the fight. "The invincible" Susan died at 86, never having gotten "a little bit of justice no bigger than that. . . . It seems so cruel."

MARCH 31, 1776 ❧ Abigail Adams writes to her husband, John: "Ladies…will not hold ourselves bound by any laws in which we have no voice…"

1792 ❧ Mary Wollstonecraft declares that females are more than domestic, sexual creatures in her book, *A Vindication of the Rights of Women*.

SEPTEMBER 1821 ❧ Emma Hart Willard opens a secondary school for girls in Troy, New York.

JULY 19–20 1848 ❧ Elizabeth Cady Stanton, Lucretia Mott, and others call for a "convention to discuss the social, civil, and religious condition and rights of Women" in the Wesleyan Chapel at Seneca Falls, New York.

1854 ❧ Mrs. Stanton fights for married women's rights to their wages and children; she addresses the New York State legislature.

1855 ❧ Lucy Stone marries and, protesting the marriage laws, keeps her maiden name.

1868 ❧ Susan B. Anthony and Mrs. Stanton begin publishing their newspaper, *The Revolution*.

1869 ❧ Women suffragists organize, forming the National Woman Suffrage Association and the more conservative American Woman Suffrage Association. They unite in 1890.

1869 ❧ Women in Wyoming Territory are granted the right to vote.

FEBRUARY 3, 1870 ❧ The 15th Amendment is ratified: All men, whatever their race or color, may vote.

1872 ❧ Victoria Woodhull runs for president. Citizen Susan B. Anthony is arrested, tried, and convicted for voting in the presidential election.

AUGUST 18, 1920 ❧ Women are granted national suffrage—the right to vote—with the 19th Amendment to the U.S. Constitution.

1923 ❧ The Equal Rights Amendment, written by Alice Paul, is introduced in Congress by Miss Paul and the National Woman's Party.

1941–1945 ❧ Millions of women, symbolized by Rosie the Riveter, work in war industries.

1963 ❧ Betty Friedan publishes *The Feminine Mystique*, and in 1966 helps form the National Organization for Women (NOW).

Dr. Mary Edwards Walker

NOVEMBER 26, 1832
Oswego, New York

FEBRUARY 21, 1919
Oswego, New York

"I wish it was understood that I wear this style of dress from the highest, the purest, and the noblest principle."

Mary Edwards was not *the* first woman in the United States to overcome cruel obstacles and complete medical school, but she was among the first. After graduating from Syracuse Medical College in 1855, she set up practice in Ohio. Later she and her new husband, Dr. Albert Miller, opened a practice together in New York. A lady doctor? People would rather be sick! Their office went out of business. After a while, so did the marriage.

Mary Edwards Walker was not *the* first woman to wear "Turkish pantaloons" under a knee-length skirt, but she and those who did truly shocked people. Onlookers stared at, ridiculed, and insulted what hardly anyone had ever seen: trousers on a female! Journalist Amelia Bloomer wrote about the right to liberate oneself from pounds of dragging skirts, wire hoops, petticoats, and corsets. This was more than a fashion statement. This was about a woman's right to be a freely walking, thinking human being instead of a ruffled doll. Years after the dress-reform crusaders of the

1850s caved in to ridicule and gave up their "Bloomers," an elderly Dr. Walker still upset the establishment by wearing pants instead of dresses. In fact, she got arrested more than once for wearing a man's dress suit, complete with bow tie and top hat.

It was her lifelong fight, but Mary Edwards Walker is not who comes to mind when you think of women's fight for equality. More likely you'd think of Susan B. Anthony and Elizabeth Cady Stanton. Mary Walker gave many a speech about it, but she wasn't *the* most famous campaigner for temperance, either. That would be Frances Willard.

Yet *all* of the reforming storms of her time are personified in courageous, idealistic Mary Walker, who'd be remarkable even if the Civil War hadn't broken out in 1861, changing millions of lives forever. She cared for soldiers in a Washington hospital, and by 1863 she had become the first female surgeon in the U.S. Army. She worked behind the battle lines, doctoring soldiers from both the Confederate and Union armies. She even did spy work.

On April 10, 1864, a Rebel sentry captured her. Dr. Walker, prisoner of war, was taken to Richmond, Virginia, the Confederate capital, and released four months later. On November 11, 1865, President Andrew Johnson awarded her the Congressional Medal of Honor, the highest military award.

After the war Mary wrote and lectured on her many ideas to improve the world, such as suffrage for women and reforming the ridiculous, unhealthful way they had to dress. She was passionately against tobacco, drinking, and tight corsets. She wore her medal on her gentlemanly black coat even after government officials decided in 1917 that she didn't deserve it. Mary said they could have it back "over my dead body." Sixty years later, President Jimmy Carter saw to it that Dr. Mary Walker, army surgeon, was an official Medal of Honor winner. No other woman has been so honored.

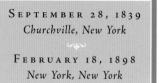

Frances E. Willard

SEPTEMBER 28, 1839
Churchville, New York

FEBRUARY 18, 1898
New York, New York

*"Sow an act and you reap a habit;
sow a habit and you reap a character;
sow a character and you reap a destiny."*

Xenophon, an ancient Greek philosopher, defined temperance like this: "Moderation in all things healthful, total abstinence from all things harmful." How could such a tame point of view lead to a mass political movement, saloons smashed into splinters, gangsters with machine guns, or an amendment to the U.S. Constitution? The campaign for temperance did, because to the campaigners—women, mostly—"all things harmful" meant alcohol.

Many of the women fighting for the right to vote and the end of slavery were passionate "teetotalers" (nondrinkers). They knew firsthand that drunkenness was a home wrecker, a society wrecker. The huge organization that led the war on drink was the Woman's Christian Temperance Union (WCTU), and its leader was Frances E. Willard. Her admirers called her a "prophetess" and the "Greatest American Woman." Others called her "the most dangerous."

Frances was an "outdoorsy" Wisconsin girl who became the president of a women's college in Evanston, Illinois. At about the same time, praying, hymn-singing "Woman Crusaders" were marching into saloons in New York and Ohio, begging bartenders to close up shop. Soon the WCTU was formed in Cleveland, Ohio. Frances E. Willard, its second president, built it into a national, then international organization.

Miss Willard had a lot more on her mind than whiskey. Behind her spectacles, her blue eyes blazed with determination to "do everything" to reform the fast-changing world. Hard times had driven rural folks from their farms. American cities were crowded with people seeking a better life. People were drowning their misery in saloons. Out West, Carry A. Nation had an answer for that. In the 1890s, this hands-on temperance worker started smashing taverns with her hatchet. "Hatchetation," she called it.

In every state in the Union, Frances made eloquent speeches against drinking, prostitution, and nasty books. She urged people to clean up their habits, their cities, and their prisons. She called for educating children instead of working them twelve hours a day in mines and factories. She pushed for fairness in the workplace and no shopping on Sundays. Every woman, she argued, needed the "ballot as a weapon of protection to her home." Soon Frances had an army of 150,000 earnest women wearing white ribbons of purity and yellow ribbons for suffrage.

In the last years of Miss Willard's life, she lectured, helped start the National Council of Women, and wrote a shelf full of books. Her work and the work of her followers eventually led to the passing of the 18th Amendment in 1919: the making, selling, or transporting of alcohol was a federal crime from 1930 to 1933. Did some folks try to get around the law in all kinds of criminal ways? Indeed they did! In 1933, "Prohibition" was undone, but that was long after Frances Willard had died, at the age of 58. The social improvements she inspired were the groundwork for the great work in progress: America.

Mary E. Lease

SEPTEMBER 11, 1853
Ridgway, Pennsylvania

OCTOBER 29, 1933
Callicoon, New York

"Wall Street owns the country. When I get through with the silk-hatted easterners, they will know that the Kansas prairies are on fire!"

I n 1893, thousands of Americans visited the Chicago World's Fair. One of the attractions was the fiery "Patrick Henry in petticoats." Her enemies called her "Yellin' Mary Ellen, the Kansas Pythoness." She was black-haired, blue-eyed, golden-voiced Mary E. (for Elizabeth, actually) Lease, one of the most famous American women in the last years of the 19th century, a time of economic trouble.

Mary learned all about trouble out in Kansas. Mary Clyens went West as a schoolteacher and eventually married Charles Lease. They and millions of other farmers might have done all right if only there'd been more rain and fewer blizzards and grasshoppers. If only crop prices weren't so low and the railroads didn't charge so much to store grain and cotton. If only bankers didn't demand so much extra money when farmers tried to pay back loans they'd borrowed for seed. Worn-out, bitter ex-homesteaders put signs on their East-bound covered wagons: IN GOD WE TRUSTED; IN KANSAS WE BUSTED.

Mr. Lease went to work in a Wichita drugstore. His wife started studying law books propped up over her washtub. The harder she scrubbed, the harder she thought. The U.S. was rich and its land was fertile, but farmers were poor. Smoke blossomed out of the factory chimneys of the world's leading industrial power, but workers were poor. A wealth of ore and coal was being dug out of the earth, but miners were poor. Where was the money? Invested in railroads, factories, and mines— and lining the pockets of the very few men who owned them. They bribed fat-cat politicians who made sure the law stayed on the side of big business.

Mary's thoughts spun right along with the political tornado that was spinning across the land: Farmers and workers were forming unions—why not a third political party? A People's Party that would fight for a more honest government, one that would see people got what they needed to live decent lives. Folks wanted the U.S. Treasury to print and mint more money. It wouldn't be worth as much, but, they figured, there'd be more of it. This political tornado, which blew many a man into office in the election of 1892, was called Populism. The best-known voice of the Populist movement was lawyer Mary E. Lease. She had discovered her gift for putting the anger of the common people into words. "We are for humanity against the corporations—for perishing flesh and blood against the money bags!"

All across the land, black-clad Mary whipped people up with her passionate opinions on temperance, woman suffrage, and fairness for farmers. The words for which she is most famous may not have been hers: "What you farmers need is to raise less corn and more hell!" She certainly thought it "was a right good piece of advice," though.

The People's Party faded away, but its ideas were still in the wind. Mary E. Lease, the "mellowed" radical, lived to see them blowing and whirling full force. Nearly all became reality in the Depression years of the 1930s.

Ida Bell Wells-Barnett

JULY 16, 1862
Holly Springs, Mississippi

MARCH 25, 1931
Chicago, Illinois

*"One had better die fighting
against injustice than die like
a dog or rat in a trap."*

On December 6, 1865, when the passing of the 13th Amendment made slavery illegal, Jim Wells and his wife, Lizzie, must have rejoiced. Their feisty three-year-old daughter, Ida, would not spend her life in bondage as they had.

Ida studied hard at a school for freed slaves in her hometown of Holly Springs. She was away visiting her grandma when she learned that fever had struck her parents. By the time she got home, they and her baby brother were dead. Sixteen-year-old Ida, determined to take care of her other brothers and sisters, became a schoolteacher.

On a spring day in 1884, Ida took the train, as usual, to her school in Woodstock, Tennessee. The conductor asked her to leave the ladies' car so white passengers would not have to sit with a black person. It took two other men to help him force the humiliated Ida past jeering passengers. Ida sued the railroad for discrimination. She was awarded five hundred dollars—a judgment that was later overturned in the state supreme court. Ida was disappointed, yes—but discouraged? No.

Ida began talking and writing about her experience with the railroad and about harsh "Jim Crow" laws that kept blacks downtrodden in the Deep South. Eventually Ida B. Wells, part-time journalist, became part owner of a newspaper, the *Free Speech and Headlight*. She wrote about courtrooms where blacks were unfairly tried and harshly punished for small crimes. When Ida described the shabby, poorly equipped schools for black children, she lost her teaching job. The next year, 1892, when three of her friends lost their lives, Ida undertook the fight for which she is best known: her crusade to end lynching.

An angry white mob stormed the Memphis jail where the three black business-men were being held (on a false charge, it turned out), dragged them out, and hanged them. It wasn't enough for Ida to comfort their widows and fatherless children. She began gathering and publishing evidence, at the risk of her own life, to make Americans face the reality of these terrible crimes. Between 1884 and 1894, she wrote, "over one thousand black men, women, and children have met this violent death. . . ."

Fearing for her safety, Ida went to work on a newspaper in New York City. She took her message to Great Britain and helped form anti-lynching societies on both sides of the Atlantic. Ida eventually settled in Chicago, where lawyer Ferdinand Barnett hired her to write for his newspaper. Soon the two activists formed a part-nership and marriage. Ida B. Wells-Barnett hyphenated her last name—in her day, a radical act of bold independence— and took over the paper.

Jim and Lizzie's Ida never lost her feistiness. As an educator, journalist, activist, and founder of the first black women's suffrage group, she devoted the last thirty years of her life to making a dream come true: the dream of Americans working side by side in equality and justice.

Jane Addams

SEPTEMBER 6, 1860
Cedarville, Illinois

MAY 21, 1935
Chicago, Illinois

"If it is natural to feed the hungry and care for the sick, it is certainly natural to give pleasure to the young, comfort to the aged, and to minister to the deep-seated craving for social intercourse that all men feel."

ig cities were full of poor folks who'd come from rural places around the world. Most wealthy people told themselves that there had always been poor people and always would be. But a few agreed with Marley's Ghost when he clanked his chains and cried out to frosty-hearted Ebenezer Scrooge: "Mankind was my business!"

In the late 1800s, this mankind business was beginning to be called "social work." It was good for the people who found help and, as Scrooge learned in Charles Dickens' tale *A Christmas Carol*, it was good for the helper, too. Jane Addams' life improved dramatically when she decided to reach out to others.

Motherless since she was a baby, Jane was raised by her adored father. The crooked-backed, "ugly, pigeon-toed little girl" with the sad eyes had a big heart and high ideals. She couldn't be happy knowing that others lived in "horrid little houses" and didn't have a well-to-do father like hers, but what could she do? In her time, the doors to most professions were closed to proper young ladies. After she graduated from the Rockford Female Seminary, she began studying to be a doctor, but poor health forced her to give it up. Then her father died. Eventually, surgery mended her spine, but Jane's heart and mind were restless. How could she be useful?

Jane and her friend Ellen Gates Starr found an answer when they set sail for Europe. In a rough part of London, they discovered Toynbee Hall, the first "settlement house," a community center with classes and programs designed to improve life for the poor.

When they returned home, Jane and Ellen went into the mankind business in a crumbly old Chicago mansion. They opened the doors of Hull-House on September 18, 1889. Over the years, thousands of people found classes, citizenship programs, and vocational training there. Jane Addams found her true calling there.

She and other social work pioneers began labor unions and worked against unsafe food, dreadful poorhouses, and insane asylums. They campaigned for the first juvenile court, child welfare, workmen's compensation, public health, and votes for women. Jane joined Ida B. Wells-Barnett in the fight against racial bigotry and segregation. She supported Florence Kelley's crusade to improve working conditions in tenement sweatshops, which led to the passing of the first state laws against child labor and for an eight-hour workday.

Jane Addams raised money, wrote books, and worked hard to help the thousands of refugees that World War I created. In 1920, she celebrated her newly won right to vote by helping to form the American Civil Liberties Union. Eleven years later, the world celebrated her life when Jane Addams was awarded the Nobel Peace Prize. The Hull-House mansion is a museum now. It is a testament to the lives enriched there, including that of Jane Addams, whose mankind business goes on in community centers around the nation to this day.

Mary Harris Jones

MAY 1, 1830
Cork, Ireland

NOVEMBER 30, 1930
Silver Spring, Maryland

*"If they want to hang me,
let them hang me, but when I am
on the scaffold, I'll cry 'Freedom
for the working class!'"*

Mary Harris was born into a poor Irish family with a history of raising a ruckus. Her father, who had protested rich landlords' treatment of peasants, escaped the hangman by fleeing to Canada; then he sent for his family. So it was that Mary grew up to be a teacher in Toronto and, later, in Memphis, Tennessee, where she met a soft-spoken ironworker.

Not long after Mary married George Jones, the Civil War began. The war was barely over when a fever epidemic killed her husband and all four of their small children. Four years later, in 1871, the Great Chicago Fire took Mary's sewing business and all she owned. This was the end of Act I in the life of "Mother" Jones, the most colorful hero of the labor movement.

In the late 19th century, millionaire businessmen were determined to keep profits high by working employees long hours, often under dangerous conditions, and paying them low wages. They could get away with it because there were plenty of immigrants, freed slaves, broke farmers, and all their children, dying for work. Mary wanted to give a voice to these suffering workers. Her husband had belonged to one of America's first national trade unions (the Iron Molders, organized in 1859). Unions organized workers so they could bargain with their bosses. If the bosses wouldn't listen, then workers would all stop working. This brave last resort (no work=no pay =no food) was called a strike.

Around 340,000 workers across the nation walked off their jobs on May 1, 1886, in an effort to win an eight-hour workday instead of the customary ten to sixteen. Mary sang along with the workers: "We want to feel the sunshine/We want to smell the flowers/We're sure that God has willed it/And we mean to have eight hours." Perhaps "the government of the people" would be on their side.

No. The government turned a deaf ear. What was good for big business was good for the country. The stage was set for a deadly war of public opinion, bayonets, demonstrations, boycotts, terror, and hunger. Companies hired spies, armies of guards, and roughnecks to break up the strikes. All too often, violence was met with more bloody, fiery violence.

Mary encouraged garment and streetcar workers in New York City, textile workers in Massachusetts, steelworkers in Pennsylvania, and coal miners in several states, daring the company guards to shoot an old woman. She called the miners "her boys." They called her "Mother."

Mother Jones took jobs in Alabama textile mills to see firsthand "little gray children" as young as six working on the looms. In 1903, she led a children's march to President Theodore Roosevelt's home in Oyster Bay, New York. He refused to meet them. More than once, she was thrown in jail. In 1913, lawmen backed by a Colorado mining company locked 83-year-old Mother Jones in a rat-filled cellar for 26 days. Most of her battles failed. Though she lived a hundred years, Mary didn't live to see the labor laws change, but she had hope: "The cause of the worker continues onward. The future is in labor's strong, rough hands."

1820s ✧ Skilled workers begin their own short-lived political party, the Working Men's Party. The "Workies" demand a ten-hour workday and the end of debtors' prison.

1834 ✧ The textile "mill girls" of Lowell, Massachusetts, strike to protest wage cuts.

1859 ✧ William H. Sylvis of Philadelphia starts the National Union of Iron Molders.

1866 ✧ Sylvis organizes workers, merchants, and farmers into the National Labor Union.

1867 ✧ Oliver H. Kelley organizes farmers into the Patrons of Husbandry, aka the Grange.

1869 ✧ Philadelphia garment workers form the Noble Order of the Knights of Labor.

1877 ✧ President Hayes sends troops against striking railroad workers.

1881 ✧ Samuel Gompers organizes 250,000 wage earners into what will be the American Federation of Labor (AFL).

MAY 4, 1886 ✧ Haymarket Square, Chicago. At a huge demonstration for an eight-hour day, a bomb kills policemen and civilians.

1890s ✧ Worst employer-employee violence ever in strikes against the Carnegie Steel Company and the manufacturer of Pullman railroad cars.

1894 ✧ Labor Day becomes a national holiday.

MARCH 25, 1911 ✧ 146 young women workers are killed in a fire at the Triangle shirtwaist factory. It leads to laws for safer factories.

1933 ✧ Frances Perkins becomes Secretary of Labor and first female member of the Cabinet.

1935 ✧ The National Labor Relations Act protects workers' right to organize.

1938 ✧ Congress establishes the minimum wage (25¢ per hour) and outlaws child labor.

1947 ✧ Congress passes the Taft-Hartley Act to restrain the power of unions.

1955 ✧ The American Federation of Labor joins the Congress of Industrial Organizations (assembly-line workers): AFL-CIO.

1962 ✧ Cesar Chavez and Dolores Huerta form what will become the United Farm Workers.

1981 ✧ President Reagan ends strike of air traffic controllers, effectively undoing their union.

OCTOBER 2000 ✧ A national park is dedicated in California to honor women workers in World War II.

Margaret Sanger

SEPTEMBER 14, 1879
Corning, New York

SEPTEMBER 6, 1966
Tucson, Arizona

"No woman can call herself free who does not own and control her body."

Margaret Higgins' mother was sick. She took in washing to help her husband provide for their family. In 22 years she found out 18 times that she was going to have a baby. Seven of those babies died as their mom grew sicker, each pregnancy taking more of her strength until she died when she was only fifty years old. She was never forgotten by her eleven children, but it was Margaret especially who remembered the lesson of her mother's life.

Margaret was studying to be a nurse when she fell in love with William Sanger. After they had a baby son, she got sick with tuberculosis, the disease that had killed her mother. Margaret got better, had two more babies—and a great restlessness. She began juggling care for her children with a job as a visiting nurse in the slums of New York City. Margaret Sanger climbed dark stairways to help tired-eyed women bring babies into their world of suffering, poverty, dirt, and illness. Like the old woman who lived in a shoe, they had so many children they didn't know what to do.

Seeing such misery made Margaret a radical social reformer. "Gone forever" was the girl Mr. Sanger had married (they later divorced). Margaret Sanger had a burning cause: what if every woman could control her bearing of children? By 1914, she was writing about "birth control" in her own magazine. When she sent out copies of *The Woman Rebel*, Margaret got in trouble with the law because even mentioning contraception in the U.S. mail was a federal crime and would be until 1936. Many Americans considered it to be a taboo subject, plainly immoral and sinful. After she was arrested, her youngest child, a daughter, died. Margaret was devastated but pushed on, convinced that her efforts would improve the future for other daughters.

On October 16, 1916, in Brooklyn, New York, Margaret Sanger defied church opposition, social convention, and the law of the land to open America's first birth-control clinic. In the ten days before the police came to take struggling, shouting Margaret off to jail, more than 150 women came to her clinic to learn how to use birth control. She was tried and sent to prison for thirty days.

Margaret kept working to make it legal for doctors to give out birth-control information and methods. She promoted worldwide population control, began what became the Planned Parenthood Federation, and sought funding for doctors who later invented the contraceptive "Pill." Margaret's cause was truly a social revolution that would have stunned her mother.

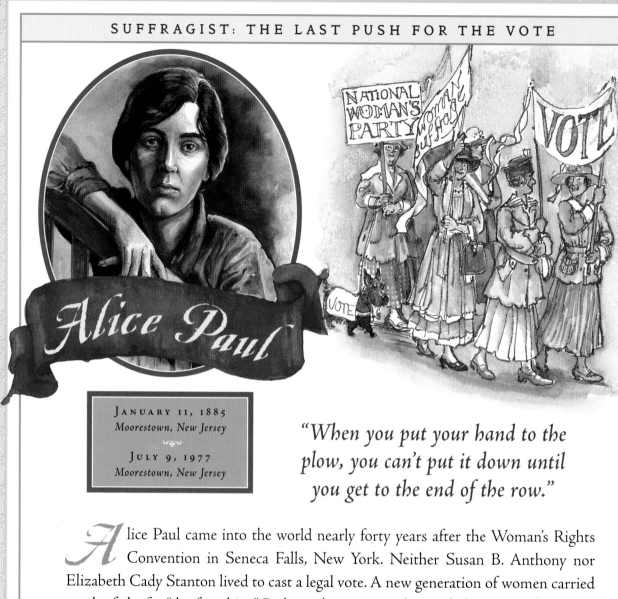

Alice Paul

JANUARY 11, 1885
Moorestown, New Jersey

JULY 9, 1977
Moorestown, New Jersey

"When you put your hand to the plow, you can't put it down until you get to the end of the row."

A lice Paul came into the world nearly forty years after the Woman's Rights Convention in Seneca Falls, New York. Neither Susan B. Anthony nor Elizabeth Cady Stanton lived to cast a legal vote. A new generation of women carried on the fight for "the franchise." Perhaps the most single-minded warrior of them all was charismatic Alice Paul.

In 1905, she graduated from Swarthmore College in Pennsylvania, then she went on to earn six more diplomas from other schools. Hungry-minded, Alice studied economics, social work, and, by 1928, earned three law degrees. She went to England, where she took time from her studies to work with the three great "suffragettes": Emmeline Pankhurst and her daughters, Sylvia and Christabel.

Instead of pleading with bored, scornful lawmakers in Parliament, they organized spectacular demonstrations and window-smashing protests. Several times they were thrown in jail, where they sometimes refused to eat. Guards tied them down and force-fed them with tubes down their throats. Alice took all she'd learned and went home to join the fight in America. She settled in Washington, D.C.

Three months later, on March 3, 1913, the day before Woodrow Wilson was to watch his inaugural parade, Alice had organized one of her own. 8,000 women marched past the White House. By 1916, Alice Paul and her followers became the National Woman's Party (NWP). They held hunger strikes, bonfires, and mass demonstrations. Day after day, "Silent Sentinels" with set faces stood at the iron fence in front of the White House, holding banners that asked such questions as MR. PRESIDENT, HOW LONG MUST WOMEN WAIT FOR LIBERTY?

Alice and other citizens of a free country were repeatedly arrested for "obstructing" the sidewalk along Pennsylvania Avenue. Though they were beaten and humiliated in jail, they did not give up. Alice, frail from force-feeding, did not give up. Tens of thousands of women of the more moderate National American Woman Suffrage Association did not give up until the 19th Amendment was finally passed in Congress in 1919. Was this victory? Yes. And no.

Thirty-six states (¾ of the 48) had to agree. In one state capitol after another, suffragists pursued and persuaded legislators, pinning yellow blossoms—the symbol of their campaign—to the politicians' lapels. With each state victory, Alice Paul stitched a star onto a banner. On August 18, 1920, 72 years after Elizabeth Cady Stanton declared women's "inalienable right to the elective franchise," a starry banner spilled over the balcony at the Woman's Party headquarters. A narrow vote in the Tennessee statehouse gave every woman, then and ever after, the victory.

Miss Paul had in mind one more little change to the law of the land: an "Equal Rights Amendment" that would make discrimination against females illegal. She wrote the words of the "ERA" in 1921, then spent the rest of her long life agitating for women's equal treatment around the world.

Eleanor Roosevelt

OCTOBER 11, 1884
New York City

NOVEMBER 7, 1962
New York City

"You gain strength, courage and confidence by every experience in which you really stop to look fear in the face.... You must do the thing you think you cannot do."

Like Jane Addams, Eleanor saw herself as "an ugly child." Her chilly mom and alcoholic dad died when she was a girl. She could identify with people who were left out and left behind. But fate—and her family's penchant for politics—put her smack in the middle of the public spotlight. Her uncle, Theodore Roosevelt, was president in 1905 when Eleanor married her distant cousin, Franklin Delano Roosevelt. By March 4, 1933, Franklin was president and Eleanor was First Lady. Life had turned them into parents of six children and very different people from those newlyweds who, if they didn't exactly live happily ever after, certainly were the most powerful, controversial political team in the 20th century.

When Franklin was crippled with polio in 1921, it looked as though his career in government was doomed. While he faced pain and uncertainty, Eleanor battled her painful self-doubts and disapproving mother-in-law to do Democratic Party work on his behalf. She was scared, but she did it anyway, and in doing so she discovered treasures she didn't know she had: energy and a steely will. She developed her gifts for writing, teaching, and organizing. In her high-pitched voice, she gave speech after speech. She helped run a school in New York City and worked to make life better for people who weren't born into a rich family as Eleanor had been. By 1928, when Franklin D. Roosevelt became governor of New York, Eleanor Roosevelt was

her own public person. From 1933 to 1945, while optimistic President "FDR" did everything he could think of to get America through hard times and war, Eleanor gave regular press conferences and wrote a daily newspaper column about her many social causes.

She worked with such educators as Mary McLeod Bethune to fight racial injustice. When the great African-American singer Marian Anderson gave her famous concert on the steps of the Lincoln Memorial, it was Eleanor who made it possible. As the "eyes and ears" for her wheelchair-bound husband, she traveled the world visiting Americans, including U.S. soldiers. She changed and expanded the job of First Lady. The death of FDR and the explosion of the atomic bomb in 1945 changed the world—forever.

Out of the ashes of World War II arose the United Nations, an organization devoted to promoting world peace. Eleanor Roosevelt represented her country there until 1952. She helped to write the Universal Declaration of Human Rights "for all peoples and all nations." Eleanor left her post at the UN (President Kennedy reappointed her to the U.S. delegation in 1961), but she continued to write, speak, and travel to promote its work. She campaigned for the Democratic Party and wrote many a book. The shy bride had become an honored and admired humanitarian and diplomat: restless Eleanor Roosevelt, citizen of the world.

Fannie Lou Hamer

OCTOBER 6, 1917
Montgomery County, Mississippi

MARCH 14, 1977
Mound Bayou, Mississippi

*"I'm sick and tired
of being sick and tired."*

There was another new baby over at the Townsends. Jim and Lou Ella's fourteen sons and five daughters had a baby sister, Fannie Lou. The Townsends were Mississippi dirt farmers, sharecroppers who bought the seeds, planted, weeded, and picked, then "shared" half the crop with the man who owned the land. "Life was worse than hard," said Fannie Lou when she grew up. "It was horrible! We never did have enough to eat."

When other children started school, Fannie Lou was out in the fields, helping her family pick cotton. Like other poor country kids, the Townsends went to school in the winter, after the harvest, then left in March, at planting time. It was a hard way to get the education that Fannie Lou craved.

Her family worked and saved and, little by little, they made progress. Eventually they had three mules and two cows—until a white neighbor poisoned the animals lest the Townsends get too high in the world. All of this and more was stored up in her memory when Fannie Lou met and married Perry "Pap" Hamer during the years when America was fighting World War II. They raised four adopted daughters while they worked very hard on a plantation near Ruleville, Mississippi.

After the war ended overseas, black Americans faced a long battle at home—for their rights as citizens. In August of 1962, Mrs. Hamer heard of a meeting over at their church about their rights as citizens to vote. She and her friends knew it would not be easy to travel down that road. Some bigots worked hard to keep things like they were in the old days, before slaves got their freedom (and little else). They terrorized blacks who "stepped out of line" with threats—and worse. Registering to vote meant risking one's life.

Fannie Lou had never known she could vote. Now that she did, nothing was going to stop her. Either she'd be killed fast, she figured, or a little at a time, as she had been all her life.

After their bus ride to the county courthouse, Fannie Lou Hamer and her neighbors ran into the same voting obstacles facing blacks all over the South: a deliberately too hard test, and a poll tax no one could afford. Fannie Lou worked, studied, and saved for months. For her efforts she was shot at, and she and her husband got fired and evicted. All of this only made Fannie Lou Hamer an unshakable activist, determined to help all black citizens join the ranks of registered voters.

At demonstration meetings, at sit-ins and in jail, she spoke out. She raised her rich voice in song to calm folks down and lift them up. Even after she was arrested and horribly beaten in a Mississippi jail, she kept working to change the laws and make life a little easier for the poor. She ran for Congress in 1964, witnessed the passage of the Voting Rights Act of 1965, which outlawed the racist obstacles she had faced, and addressed the Democratic National Convention in 1964 and again in 1968. All this and more was stored up in her memory when she died in 1977. Thanks to her and other peaceful warriors of the civil rights movement, it was a very different America.

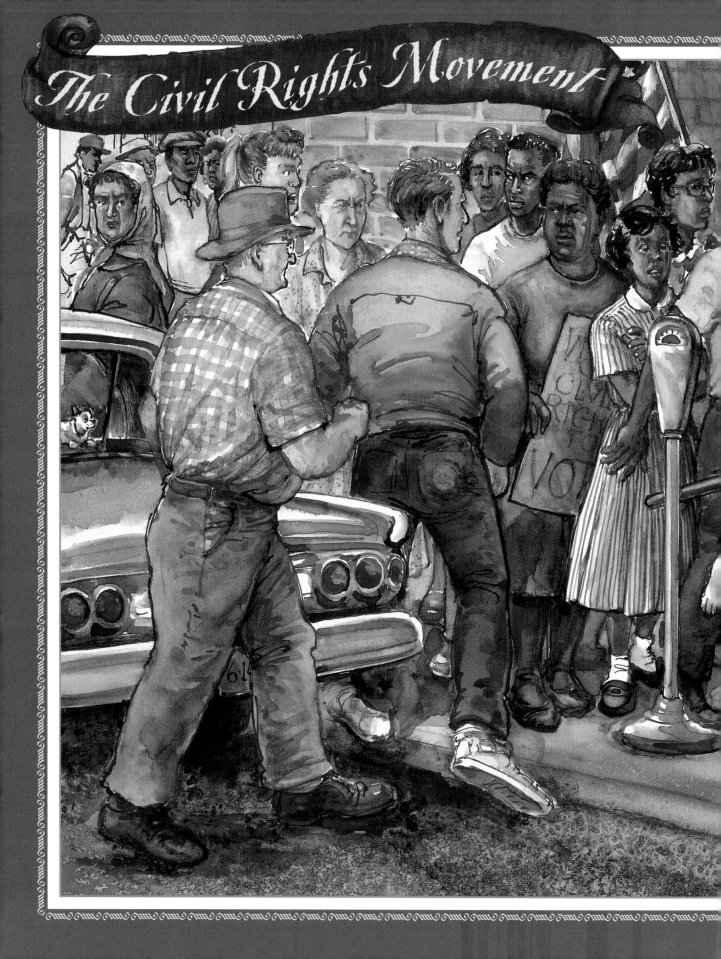

The Civil Rights Movement

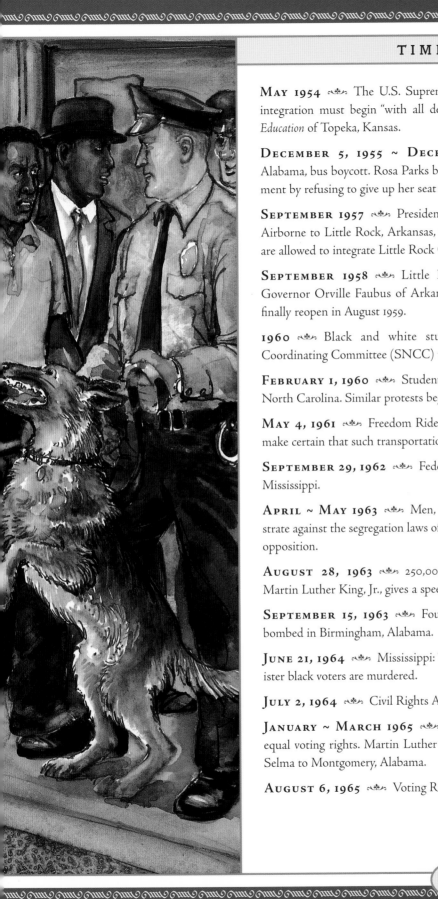

MAY 1954 ☙ The U.S. Supreme Court rules that public school racial integration must begin "with all deliberate speed" in *Brown v. the Board of Education* of Topeka, Kansas.

DECEMBER 5, 1955 ~ DECEMBER 20, 1956 ☙ Montgomery, Alabama, bus boycott. Rosa Parks becomes a symbol of the civil rights movement by refusing to give up her seat and move to the back of a city bus.

SEPTEMBER 1957 ☙ President Dwight D. Eisenhower sends the 101st Airborne to Little Rock, Arkansas, to make certain that nine black students are allowed to integrate Little Rock Central High School.

SEPTEMBER 1958 ☙ Little Rock public high schools are closed. Governor Orville Faubus of Arkansas refuses to desegregate them. They finally reopen in August 1959.

1960 ☙ Black and white students start the Student Nonviolent Coordinating Committee (SNCC) to enfranchise African-Americans.

FEBRUARY 1, 1960 ☙ Student sit-ins at a lunch counter in Greensboro, North Carolina. Similar protests begin all over the South.

MAY 4, 1961 ☙ Freedom Riders begin dangerous interstate bus rides to make certain that such transportation is integrated.

SEPTEMBER 29, 1962 ☙ Federal troops help integrate the University of Mississippi.

APRIL ~ MAY 1963 ☙ Men, women, and children march and demonstrate against the segregation laws of Birmingham, Alabama. They face violent opposition.

AUGUST 28, 1963 ☙ 250,000 people March on Washington, D.C. Martin Luther King, Jr., gives a speech: "I have a dream . . ."

SEPTEMBER 15, 1963 ☙ Four little girls are killed when a church is bombed in Birmingham, Alabama.

JUNE 21, 1964 ☙ Mississippi: Three young men who were trying to register black voters are murdered.

JULY 2, 1964 ☙ Civil Rights Act is passed.

JANUARY ~ MARCH 1965 ☙ Demonstrations in Selma, Alabama, for equal voting rights. Martin Luther King, Jr., and 30,000 people march from Selma to Montgomery, Alabama.

AUGUST 6, 1965 ☙ Voting Rights Act is passed.

Betty Friedan

FEBRUARY 4, 1921
Peoria, Illinois

*"...we learned the power
of our solidarity,
the power of our sisterhood."*

In 1775, in a letter to her husband, John, at the Continental Congress, Abigail Adams wrote: "...in the new Code of Laws which...will be necessary for you to make I desire you would Remember the Ladies. . . . If particular care and attention is not paid to the Ladies we are determined to foment a Rebellion. . . ." Nearly two hundred years later, on August 26, 1970, thousands of women "Marched for Equality" in America's cities. They had taken Abigail's words to heart, and those of another revolutionary woman: Betty Friedan.

Women had made progress since winning the right to vote in 1920. In the 1920s and 1930s, more young women than ever before attended college and began professional careers. In the 1940s, millions of women helped the United States win World War II by keeping factories and businesses running while the men fought overseas. Then, when the men returned from war, the powerful message to women was: "Go home."

During the 1950s, the high-pay, high-status jobs were reserved for men. A woman was supposed to be a happy homemaker and mommy who supported her husband's work. It was journalist Betty Friedan who put into words what women were feeling. They loved their families and homes, and yet…so many felt that their dreams were turning to dust.

Betty Friedan's book, *The Feminine Mystique* (1963), was—and still is—controversial. Betty wrote that women needed goals and mind-challenging work of their own. Moms and dads should share the important work of raising a family.

Ms. Friedan (rather than "Miss" or "Mrs.," which define a woman by her marital status) began the National Organization for Women (NOW) in 1966. Later, in 1971, she and others, such as Gloria Steinem, Shirley Chisholm, and Fannie Lou Hamer, organized the National Women's Political Caucus to get more women elected into office. Feminists have waged a long fight for the passage of a law written by Alice Paul in 1923. The Equal Rights Amendment says, "Equality of rights under the law shall not be denied…on account of sex." The Senate passed it in 1972, but the "ERA" has yet to be ratified.

The women's liberation movement inspired passionate demonstrations. There were plenty of heated discussions about marriage, girls in sports, women in church pulpits, equal pay for equal work, and the job of motherhood. When a woman uses her own credit card and pays the bill with money she earned as a TV news anchor, jet pilot, firefighter, or senator, she can thank the "bra burners" and the "libbers," as feminists were called by many who did not share their views.

The civil rights movement was needed to realize the dream of emancipation. The women's liberation movement, begun by Betty Friedan, was needed to help the suffragists' dreams come true. And one can only dream of Abigail Adams' reaction to her 20th-century sisters' "Rebellion of the Ladies."

Dolores Huerta

APRIL 10, 1930
Dawson, New Mexico

*"I think we brought to the world...
the whole idea of boycotting
as a nonviolent tactic."*

Imagine a wide, brightly lit produce aisle in a grocery store. Cool mounds of red and green grapes. Piles of fragile tomatoes, leafy lettuces, and rosy peaches. Someone picked them. Many someones stooped, climbed, reached, and picked them out in the broiling sun. As the plants grew and ripened in their seasons, workers "followed the crops" from farm to vineyard to orchard, working with nasty weed killer and bug spray. For many years, for all of this hot, strenuous, poisonous work, the families of migrant farmworkers have generally been paid very little.

In the hard 1930s, multitudes of people from the Mexican border came looking for farmwork in the fertile Southwest. Some who came to the San Joaquin Valley of California might have found free lodging at the Stockton hotel run by Dolores Huerta's mother. When Dolores grew up and became a teacher, she taught the farmworkers' thin, shoeless children—when they weren't off working in the fields. They and their parents often lived in squalid camps without electricity or running water.

In their workplaces, they were denied toilets and clean water. It was for their sake that Dolores left teaching to work with the Community Service Organization.

The CSO was begun to help poor workers in the Los Angeles barrios (Spanish-speaking neighborhoods) improve their lives, register to vote, and work for better laws. In 1951, a law was passed allowing growers to hire Mexican workers and pay them less money. Whole families might be paid twenty cents for three hours of back-breaking work. Desperate people are easily cheated.

Dolores Huerta and the brilliant CSO activist Cesar Chavez formed the National Farm Workers Association, later to be known as the United Farm Workers, in 1962. Winning fair treatment for migrant farmworkers became their mission: La Causa (The Cause).

What would it take? Years of organizing poor workers and picketing, striking against, and bargaining with the growers. They enlisted Anglo and Hispanic students, feminists, politicians, and religious activists to speak out. Besides raising eleven children, Dolores Huerta directed huge boycotts. If consumers were convinced not to buy any grapes, for instance, then the grape growers would sooner or later have to bargain with the workers. For La Causa, she was beaten. She was arrested twenty-two times. For La Causa, Cesar Chavez endured weeks of fasting. "To be a man," he said, "is to suffer for others." It took all of this and more before the governor of California signed, in 1975, the first law to protect farmworkers' right to organize and bargain for better wages, working conditions, and benefits such as medical plans.

Dolores Huerta continues to work for women's rights and for better lives for poor laborers. "I thought I could do more by organizing farmworkers," she said, "than by trying to teach their hungry children."

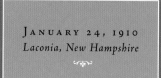

Doris Haddock

JANUARY 24, 1910
Laconia, New Hampshire

"I have been involved in reform fights most of my adult life, but I saved the most important for last—the fight to establish true democracy in this country."

The United States is not a monarchy: no kings or queens here. It's not a dictatorship, in which a powerful bigshot tells everyone what to do, and it was never meant to be an oligarchy, in which a few powerful people run the country. The revolutionary idea at the heart of our nation is that the power of government is held by the citizens. As we vote and elect representatives, "we the people of the United States" participate in governing ourselves.

It is this idea that inspired a retired secretary from New Hampshire to set out from the Pacific Coast and go for a walk on New Year's Day, 1999. By the time she finished her walk, the whole country knew about Doris Haddock, aka "Granny D," and the idea behind the words on the yellow flag she carried: NATIONAL CAMPAIGN FINANCE REFORM.

Every election, campaigns cost more money. The cost of advertising on the public airways forces most candidates to ask for millions of dollars from companies, groups with particular goals, and rich individuals, who then expect (and usually get) special treatment in the law. In order to be reelected, politicians have to spend their time raising the necessary cash. This means that people with good ideas and no money may not get elected in the first place. This means that democracy can be bought and sold. Some say people should be free to spend as they choose in order to communicate ideas. But "if money is speech," said Doris, "then those with more money have more speech. . . . It makes us no longer equal citizens." This means that unless there are laws to change the way elections are run, the whole idea of the nation is spoiled.

Doris Haddock, a five-foot-tall great-grandma, was no stranger to citizenship. She performed one-woman feminist plays in the 1930s. In 1960, she, her husband, and five others drove clear to Alaska to demonstrate against the testing of hydrogen bombs. After her dear husband and best friend both died, Doris decided to do "a great thing" for the American ideal of self-governance: "because it is our dream and our history." She would protest the selling of the government to big corporations and billionaires. She would encourage people to *be* the government—not merely its customers.

Granny D's yellow flag fluttered behind her as she trekked through deserts, skied through blizzards, made remarkable speeches on statehouse steps, and walked ten miles a day, 3,200 miles in all, to Washington, D.C. Along the way, high school bands played for her, mayors gave her the key to their cities, and people cheered, "Go, Granny, Go!" On February 29, 2000, more than 2,000 citizens joined her in the last mile to the U.S. Capitol. On the marble steps ninety-year-old Doris Haddock said, "Here we are, senators, at your doorstep: We the people.... How did you dare think that we would not come here to these steps to denounce your corruptions in the name of all who have given their lives to our country's defense and improvement."

Her long walk is done, her grand book about it is written, but her fight goes on. On April 21, 2000, Doris and fellow activists were arrested—for unlawful assembly— while she was reading aloud the Declaration of Independence under the dome of the Capitol. Campaign reform legislation is, at this writing still being wrangled over by our elected representatives.

"It's never too late to do something great."
—DORIS HADDOCK

What can you do to change the world?

1. What's the matter? There are so many problems. Disease. Violence. Soiled environment. Unfairness. War. Someone's hungry. Someone needs to know how to read. What touches you, makes you mad? Awakens your heart? Knocks on your door?

2. Study your problem. For almost every big problem there is an organization, Web sites, books. If it's a neighborhood or school problem, has it been written about in the newspaper? Find individuals who might have an answer. Check with your library and/or your local government.

3. How could what's wrong be made right? Do people need to know about the problem? Should letters be written to the newspaper or to your elected representative? Does money need to be raised? Does a law need to be passed? Are volunteers needed?

RESOURCES

Some handy addresses:

http://www.grannyd.com
*(an excellent site with plenty
of citizen-participation resources)*

The White House
1600 Pennsylvania Avenue
Washington, D.C. 20500
president@whitehouse.gov

*If you would like to contact your
congressional representative online:*
The House of Representatives:
http://www.house.gov
The Senate: http://www.senate.gov

Girls, Inc. *(a girl-empowering organization)*
30 East 33rd Street
New York, NY 10016
http://www.girlsinc.org

Kids Voting USA *(Be the government!)*
398 South Mill Avenue, Suite 304
Tempe, Arizona 85281
http://www.kidsvotingusa.org

Free the Children International
16 Thornbank Road
Thornhill, Ontario, Canada L4J 2A2
http://www.freethechildren.org
*(Started by twelve-year-old Craig Kielburger
to end the worldwide practice of child slavery.)*

PLACES TO VISIT

Little Rock Central High School
(National Historic Site)
2125 West Daisy L. Gatson Drive
Little Rock, AR 72202-5211

National Civil Rights Museum
450 Mulberry Street
Memphis, TN 38103-4214

Susan B. Anthony House
17 Madison Street
Rochester, NY 14608

Women's Rights National Historic Park
136 Fall Street
Seneca Falls, NY 13148

GLOSSARY

agitator someone who wants to stir people up for a cause

anarchist someone who believes in anarchy—the absence of rules. Emma Goldman (1869–1940) was a famous anarchist who believed that organized government squashed individual liberty.

blacklist a list of those who shall not be hired because of their beliefs or actions

boycott to join with others in refusing to purchase products or a service, or to patronize a store where there are unfair dealings

feminist someone who believes that women should be treated equally

manifesto an important public declaration of what should be done and why

pacifist someone who is opposed to violence or war. Reformers such as Jane Addams, Dolores Huerta, and Martin Luther King, Jr., adopted the nonviolent methods for social change that were developed by the great pacifist of India, Mohandas K. Gandhi.

republic a nation in which the power rests with the citizens

scab an insulting name for someone who, for whatever reason, takes the place of a striking worker

socialism the idea that government, rather than individuals, should own and control the nation's resources. Many reformers, such as Margaret Sanger and Frances Willard, who were frustrated with how things were in America in the early 20th century, adopted socialist views.

BIBLIOGRAPHY

Campion, Nardi Reeder. *Ann the Word*. Boston: Little, Brown and Company, 1976.

Flagler, John J. *The Labor Movement in the United States*. Minneapolis: Lerner Publications Co., 1990.

Haddock, Doris, and Dennis Burke. *Granny D: Walking Across America in My 90th Year*. New York: Villard, 2001.

Rubel, David. *Fannie Lou Hamer: From Sharecropping to Politics*. New Jersey: Silver Burdett Press, 1990.

Stanley, Jerry. *Big Annie of Calumet*. New York: Crown Publishers, 1996.

Stiller, Richard. *Queen of the Populists: The Story of Mary Elizabeth Lease*. New York: Thomas Y. Crowell, 1970.

Turner, Glennette Tilley. *Follow in Their Footsteps*. New York: Cobblehill Books, 1997.

FURTHER READING

Catch the Spirit: Teen Volunteers Tell How They Made a Difference, by Susan K. Perry (Franklin Watts)

Fund Raising, by Irene Cumming Kleeberg (Franklin Watts)

Girls Who Rocked the World, by Amelie Welde (Gareth Stevens Publishing)

I Can Save the Earth, by Anita Holmes (Julian Messner)

The Kid's Guide to Social Action, by Barbara A. Lewis (Free Spirit Publishing)

Kids with Courage: True Stories About Young People Making a Difference, by Barbara A. Lewis (Free Spirit Publishing)

Take a Stand, by Daniel Weizmann (Price Stern Sloan)

The Declaration of Independence, by Thomas Jefferson et al.

The United States Constitution